D1472269

AN ORIGIN STORY

Based on the Marvel comic book series Spider-Man
Adapted by Rich Thomas
Interior Illustrated by The Storybook Art Group
Jacket & Case Illustrated by Pat Olliffe and Brian Miller

New York

marvelkids.com

TM & © 2011 Marvel & Subs.

Published by Marvel Press, an imprint of Disney Book Group. No part of this book may be reproduced or transmitted in any form or by any means, electronic or mechanical, including photocopying, recording, or by any information storage and retrieval system, without written permission from the publisher. For information address Marvel Press, 114 Fifth Avenue, New York, New York 10011-5690.

Jacket and Case Illustrated by Pat Olliffe and Brian Miller
Designed by Winnie Ho

Printed in the United States of America
3 5 7 9 10 8 6 4
G942-9090-6-12079
ISBN 978-1-4231-4317-8

Have you ever felt lonely? Sad? *Powerless?*

Peter Parker felt that way every day. He was a
student at Midtown High. Some of the other kids at
school didn't understand why Peter enjoyed the things
he did. And sometimes when kids don't understand
something, they can act cruelly.

Peter enjoyed all his classes, but **science was his favorite.** He was the best student Midtown High had seen in many years, and his teachers were very proud of him.

The only thing Peter loved more than science was his family. He lived with his Aunt May and his Uncle Ben in Queens, New York. And whenever Peter felt **sad at school**, he remembered he'd be home soon and he'd **start to smile**.

Even though some of the kids at school didn't like him, **Peter never stopped trying to be friendly.** He had heard about a great demonstration at the Science Hall. He asked the other kids if they wanted to join him.

The other students just laughed at Peter. One of them, a bully named Flash Thompson, even **pushed him to the ground.**

By the time Peter arrived at the Science Hall, he had forgotten all about his classmates' cruel actions. All he could think about was the experiment. He couldn't wait to see how the scientists would control a **radioactive wave!**

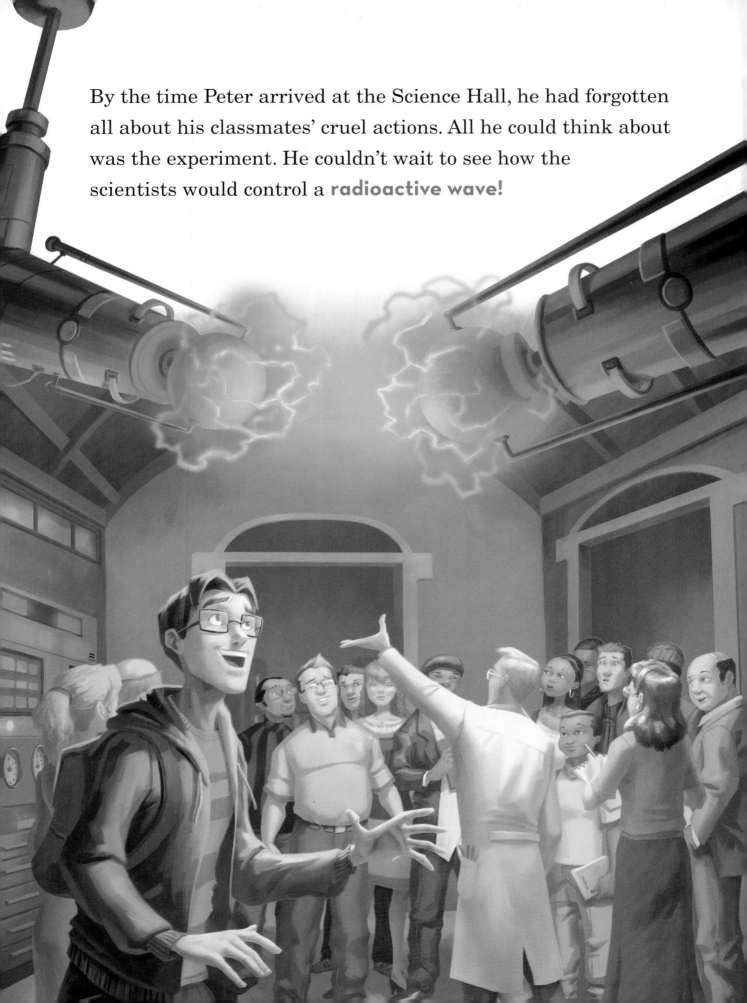

The rays were ready.

Peter eagerly looked on. **But so did something else.** The demonstration was about to begin!

Peter was awed by the experiment. He was thrilled to be there, in the company of such brilliant scientists. He wanted to be just like them—**smart, talented . . . amazing!**

Everyone was so fascinated that no one noticed when something unplanned occurred. A **spider** descended between the rays just as they were activated.

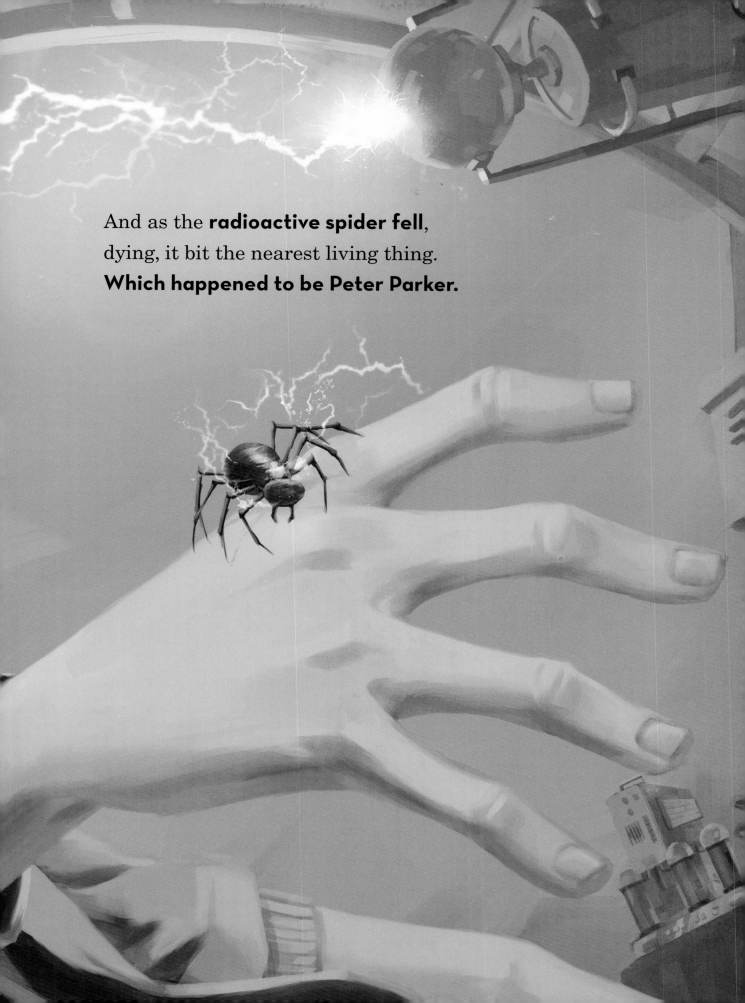

And as the **radioactive spider fell**, dying, it bit the nearest living thing. **Which happened to be Peter Parker.**

As soon as he was bitten, Peter felt weak and tired. **The room begin to spin.** The scientists noticed that Peter looked ill, and they offered to help him.

But Peter just wanted to get out of the dark laboratory and into the fresh air.

Peter felt a **sudden, peculiar tingling** in his head. It was an itching, urging, nagging feeling. The only thing he understood about it was that he was meant to **react**.

To do
something.

So he did.

Peter was sure he was **dreaming.**

He couldn't really be **climbing** up a wall. Nobody could do that.

When he reached the roof, he grabbed on to a chimney— and **crushed** it! He didn't have that kind of strength.

Peter felt the tingly feeling again. This time it gave him the urge to spring. And so he **jumped** from one tall roof to another.

And when he wanted to go back down to the street, the same strange feeling told him the easiest way to get there was to **climb down** a clothesline.

Peter stared at himself in amazement. **How could this be happening?**

Then, Peter realized he had started feeling different right after being bitten by that spider in the lab. Somehow the experiment must have affected the dying creature. **And when it bit Peter, it transferred its power to him!**

As he wandered home, amazed and half-dazed, a sign outside an old wrestling theater caught his eye. It would be the perfect way to test all of his **newfound abilities.**

Peter rushed home.

And then he rushed
right back.

Peter was ready to test his new powers on a brutish wrestler called Crusher Hogan. **Peter wore a disguise** so that no one would make fun of him if his plan didn't work.

He'd been teased and taunted enough. When Peter challenged him, **Crusher Hogan** laughed.

But Crusher soon found that
he was **very wrong** to do so.

Peter was paid well for the victory. A man in the crowd even asked him if he'd want to be on TV. **Things finally seemed to be going right for Peter.**

Plus, Peter had his Aunt May and Uncle Ben at home. They were still doing everything they could to make him happy. His uncle had even saved up for a **special microscope** that Peter had wanted.

With his new microscope, Peter's experiments would be better than ever. Uncle Ben reminded him that knowledge and science were power. "And," Uncle Ben told Peter, "**with great power comes great responsibility.**"

Peter was too excited to settle down. He used his new microscope, his chemistry set, and his knowledge of science to create a very special **fluid.**

It had the strength and stickiness of a spider's silk. Then he created devices that could spin the fluid into a web the same way a spider would. **He called them his web-shooters.**

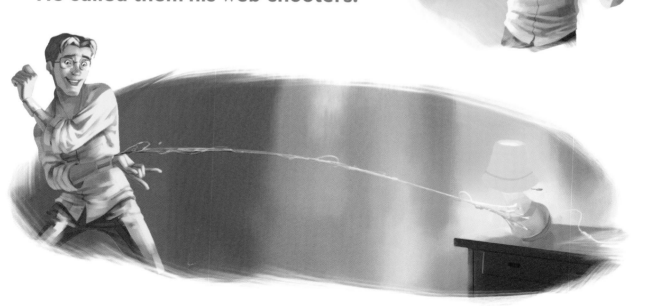

Finally, he designed a sleek new costume. Now all he needed was a stage name. **He arrived at one as good as any other. . . .**

SPIDER-MAN!

Peter's TV appearances were a huge hit.

After all, who wouldn't be amazed by a Spider-Man climbing up walls and swinging from his own webs?

Soon everyone wanted a piece of Spider-Man. Peter was starting to feel **important, wanted . . . and powerful.**

No one would ever be able to push him around again— not when he had powers like these.

Peter got lost thinking about how wonderful his new life would be. He daydreamed about fame and celebrity. And when a security guard called for help down the studio hall, Peter **ignored** him.

The crook that the guard was chasing **raced** into an elevator.

The doors closed and the thief **escaped.**

But Peter didn't care. He had **great power.** And from now on, he only needed to look out for one person—**himself.**

It didn't take long for Peter to forget about the officer and the escaped criminal. In fact, by the time he got home they were the furthest things from his mind. He was just happy to be with the **people who loved him.**

And in his spare time, when he was not studying or home with his family, Peter went out as the **famous, spectacular Spider-Man!**

But one night on his way home from a TV performance, Peter arrived to find something **worrisome.**

Peter knew something was **terribly wrong,** and he was right. His Uncle Ben had been killed by a criminal. The police officers told Peter not to worry. They had the crook cornered at an old waterfront warehouse.

Peter **ran upstairs,**

put on his costume,

and swooped over the city to avenge his uncle.

Peter was **quicker and more furious** than ever before.

At last, Peter arrived at the warehouse.

He landed on the far wall.
The thief was stunned.

And that's when **Spider-Man sprung into action!**

The crook's hat flew from his head, and Peter finally took a good look at him. Peter felt a heavy weight in his chest. It couldn't be. But it was. The man who had killed his uncle was the **same man** he allowed to escape into the elevator at the studio.

If only Peter had stopped him then! If only he had not acted so selfishly!

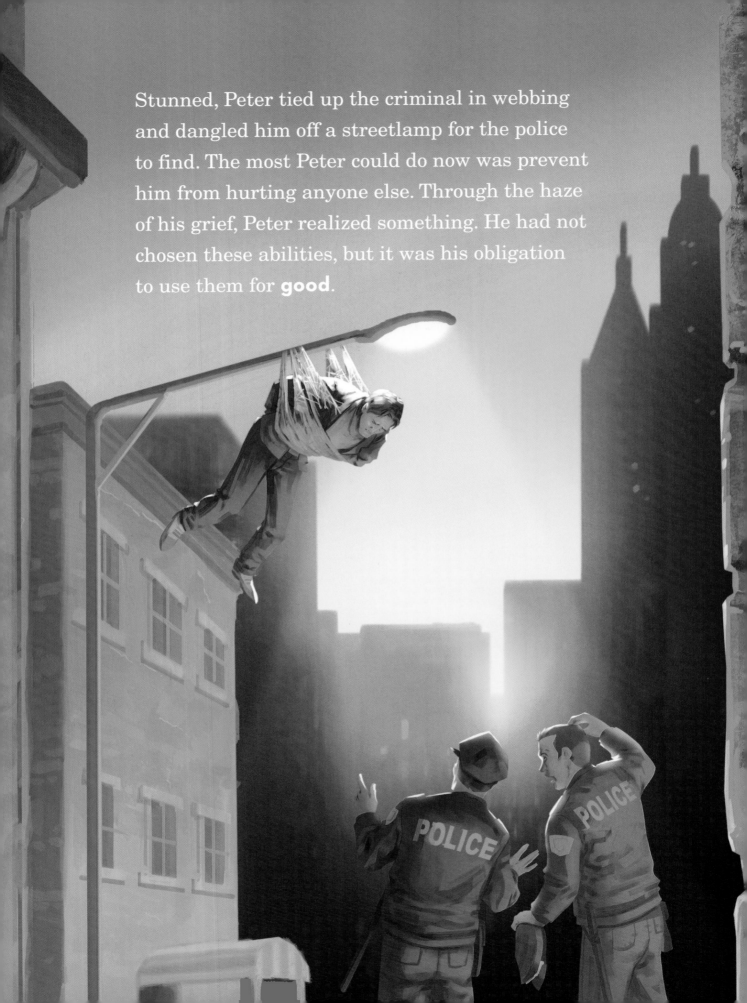

Stunned, Peter tied up the criminal in webbing and dangled him off a streetlamp for the police to find. The most Peter could do now was prevent him from hurting anyone else. Through the haze of his grief, Peter realized something. He had not chosen these abilities, but it was his obligation to use them for **good**.

It was not about money or fame or any of the other rewards his power could give him. He had finally realized that what his Uncle Ben had told him was true:

with great power comes great responsibility.

And that was the rule that Peter Parker lived by from that day forward.

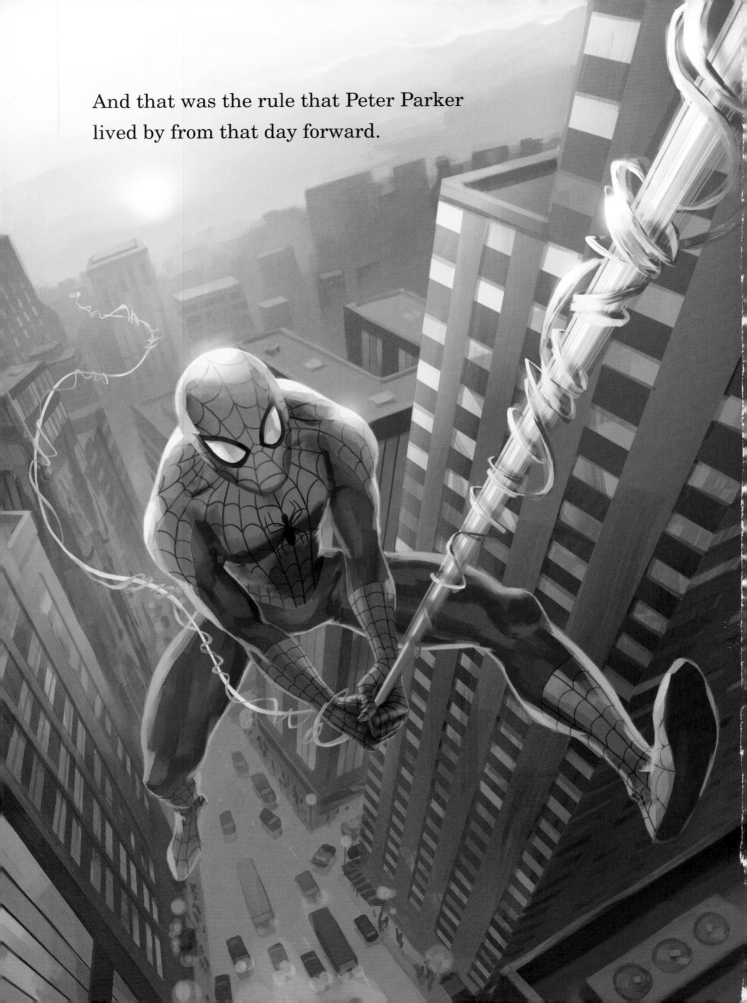